AMBITIOUS
CONSISTENCY
ENDURANCE
FOCUS
GENUINE
GRACIOUS
GUIDANCE
LEGACY
MANIFEST
MOGUL
PLAN
SISTERHOOD
SUCCESS
THRIVE

ALWAYS DO YOUR BEST.

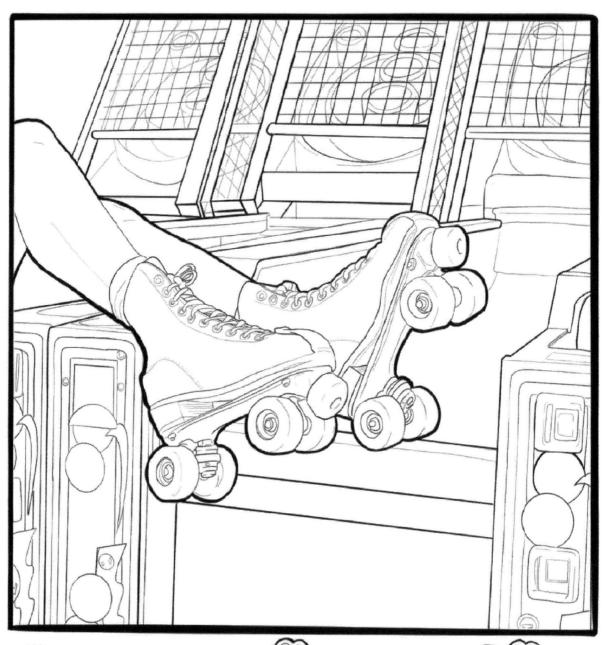

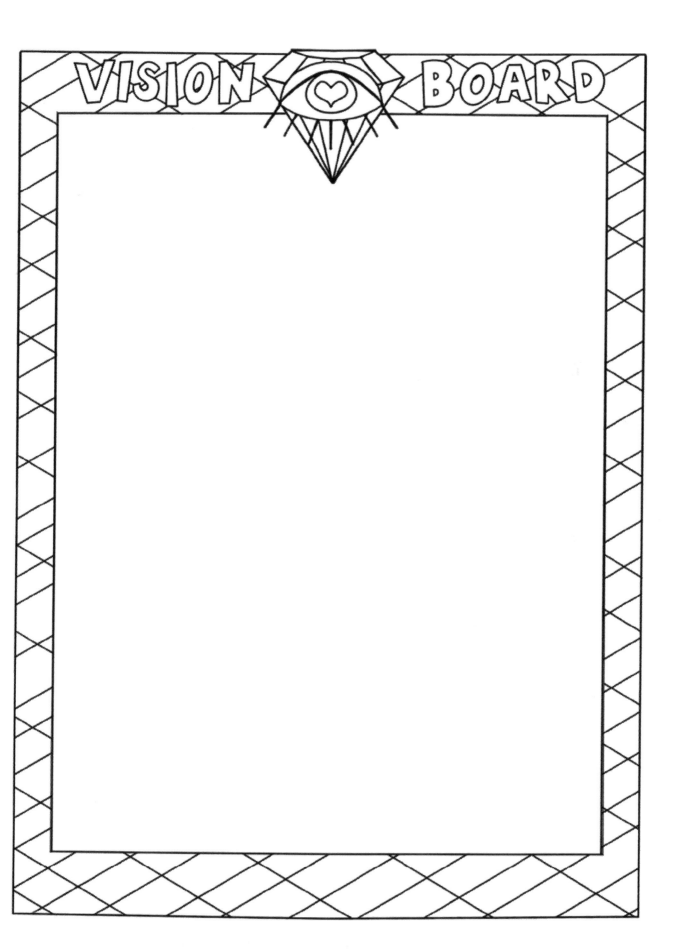

WHAT YOU

IMAGINE,

YOU BECOME.

What you think, You can CREATE!

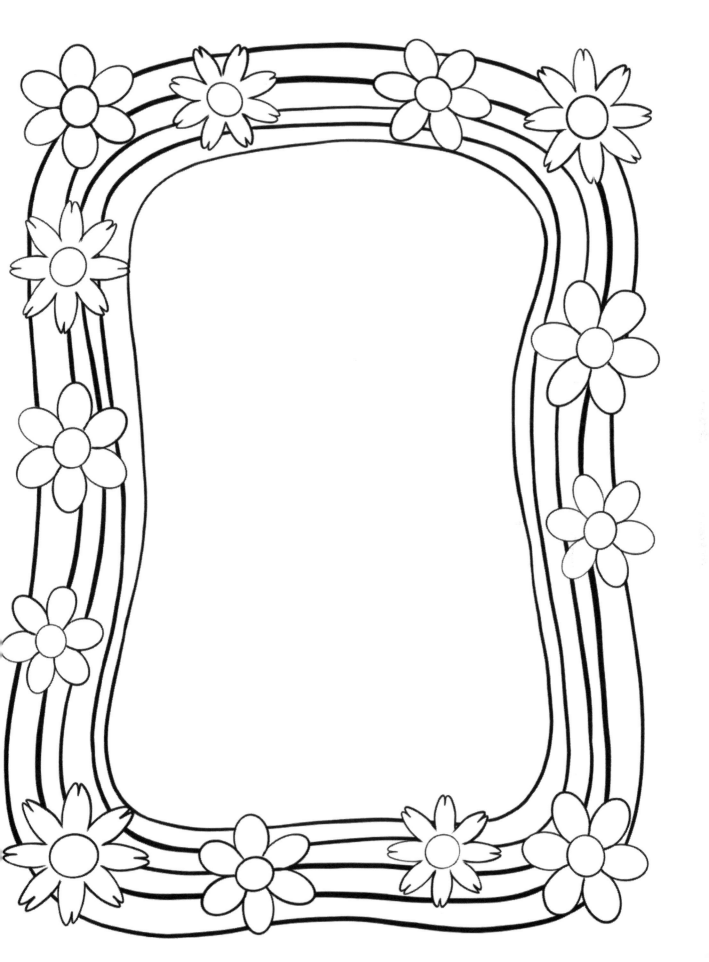

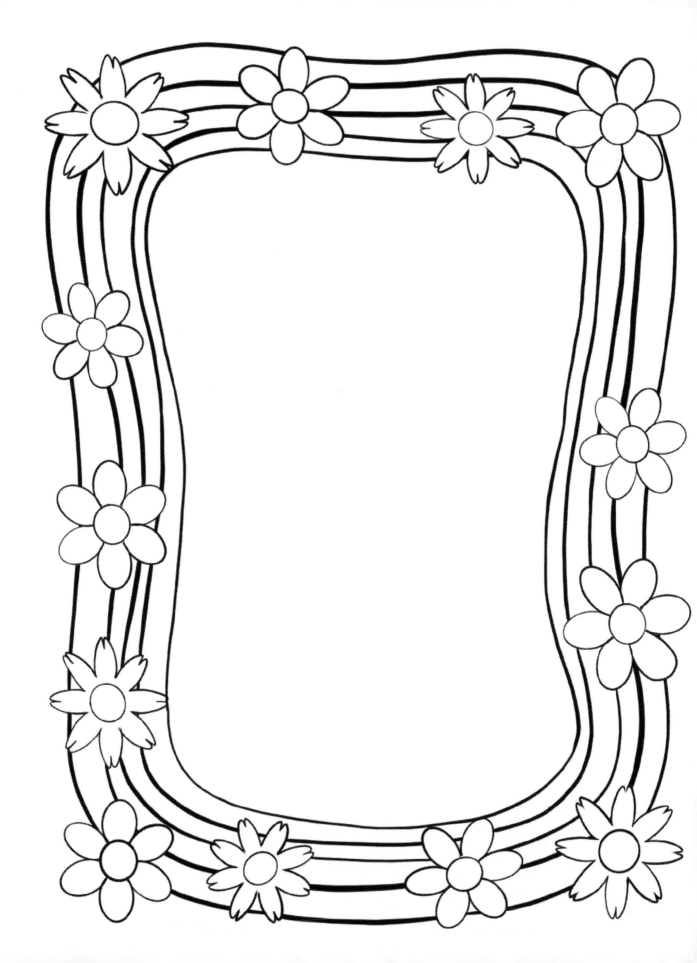

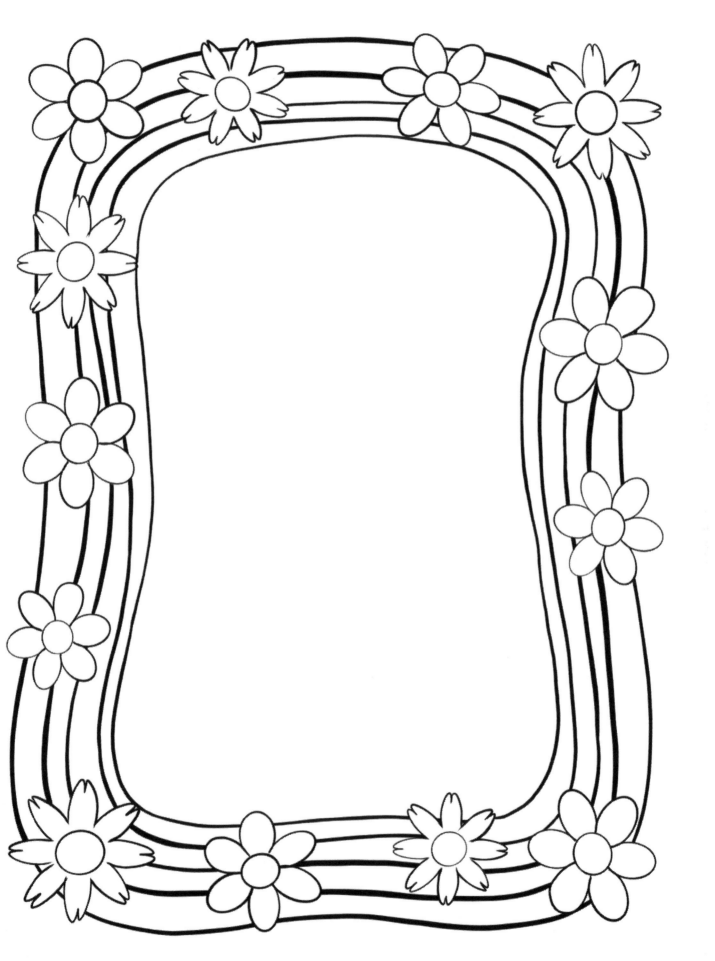

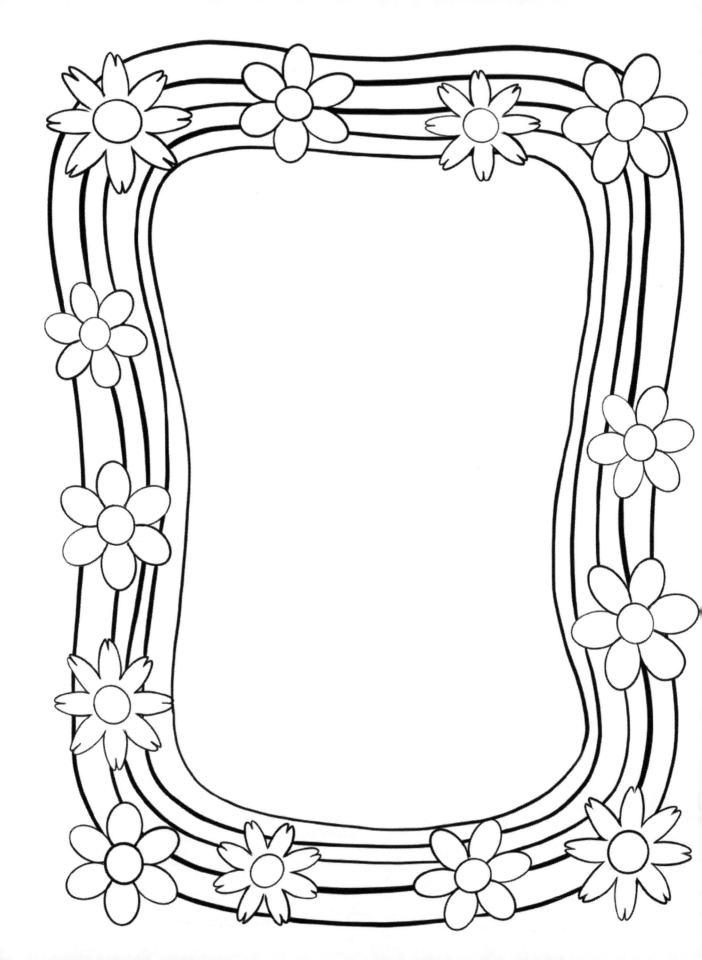

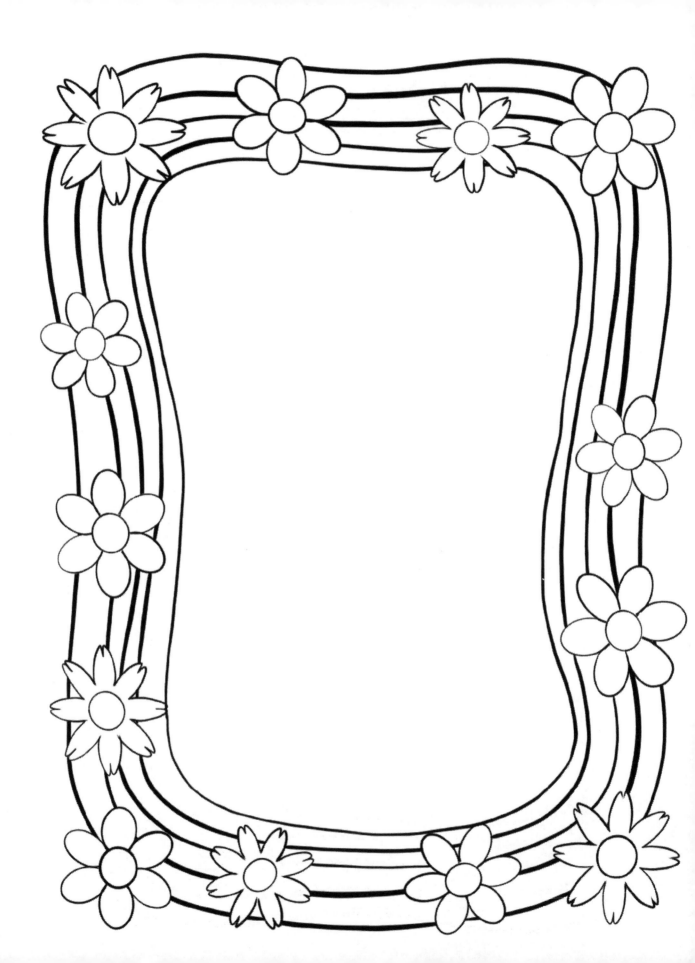

Made in the USA
Middletown, DE
22 February 2023

25319907R00024